The Band Bully

W. Derek Ratliff

Illustrations by C. Alexander Designs

ISBN: 978-1-7359820-0-7

DEDICATION

This is for all of us, young and old, who have ever been bullied and survived, and those of us still being bullied in some form or fashion.

Ring!!!!   Ring!!! Screams Mr. Alarm Clock.

"Time to get up, Kered!" Calls mom very sweet and song
like.

"Kered? Keredddd??? KERED!!!!" Mom was very sharp
and to the point!

Waking up was hard to do for Kered, because everyday it
meant having to go to a place he didn't want to go. A very
sad and terrible place ...

SCHOOL!!!!!!!!!!!!!!!!!

NOOOO!!!!!!!!!!

Brush
those
teeth!

Take a bath!!!!

Get dressed!!!

Eat breakfast!!!

"Have a great day!" Mom says as she kisses her children goodbye.

First Kimberly, the oldest.

Then Nicole, the middle child.

But Kered, the youngest stays behind. "Kered, we go through this every day. Why don't you want to go to school? Surely 6th grade isn't that bad." Mom says.

"Oh yes it is! I just don't like it!"

"But you have to go. You have things to learn so you can grow up and be very smart. Now, come on. The bus is here."

Mom sends Kered off with a kiss, but he drags his feet to the bus.

So, as soon as Kered arrived at school, this is what was waiting for him:

"Hey, sissy! Sissy boy! Kered is a sissy! Look! It's Karen!"

You see, the name calling was the reason that Kered hated school. And all of this came from a big, rough-looking, mean-looking kid named Tony! He was the biggest kid in 6th grade!!

Can you imagine if someone was picking on you all day? You wouldn't like it would you?

All day poor Kered had to hear this, but with no teachers
around, of course. And Tony wouldn't dare say these
things in front of Kered's sisters.

And all of this teasing made Kered very, very sad.

Over time, Kered became so sad that he didn't want to play outside with his sisters or his friends.

Plus he couldn't sleep.

It got so bad that he couldn't even eat. And Kered
LOVED to eat!

Has this ever happened to you or to someone you know???

Well, his parents did notice, but every time they would ask
Kered about it, he would give the same answer:

"Nothing is wrong."

One day at school as Tony began bullying Kered AGAIN
for the 20th millionth, gazillionth time, something
happened.

"Here comes the sissy! Here comes Karen!"

"Leave me alone!" Screamed Kered.

"Or what?" Snarled Tony. You're not gonna do anything,
Scary Kerry!"

Tony then shoved Kered hard against the wall, laughing as
he walked away. Kered stood there a moment almost in
tears. He really, really wanted to cry!

Then he looked up and saw that he was shoved up against a bulletin board with a notice that read:

"Want to join the band? All instruments needed. Sign up TODAY!!"

'Hey, my sister, Nicole, is in the band!

And this can be my chance to be free of Tony!'

Later that night at dinner, a very happy and enthusiastic Kered told his family. They hadn't seen Kered this excited about anything in months. He was so excited, that he had second helpings of EVERYTHING! Everyone thought it was a marvelous idea for him to join the band. Well, that is everyone except Kimberly.

"Oh great. More noise." Kimberly stated.

Everyone laughed. Well, everyone except current band member Nicole.

But which instrument to choose. Clarinet – like Nicole maybe?? But then Kered thought it had too many holes for fingers. Kered didn't know how Nicole played that thing.

Flute – the same thing, too many holes.

Saxophone would be cool. But again too many places to put your fingers.

Kered began to think 'what is up with the woodwind instruments with all of the places to put your fingers??'

Drums – too loud – definitely not. Kimberly thought there was noise before. Ha! With the drums, watch out!

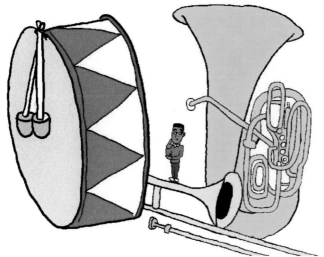

The trombone – too big, too long, just too much. So, no.

Tuba – definitely too big. So, definitely no!

The trumpet – hmmm

Well, it only has three button-like things – called valves. And it is easy to carry and loud without being too loud. It was just right.

PERFECT! Bet Tony wouldn't call Kered a sissy anymore.

So, the trumpet it is!!!

The next day at school, Kered signed up for band. Within a couple of days, his parents bought his trumpet.

The first day of band was going to be next week, and Kered was more than ready to start!

Kered could barely eat!
Or sleep.

BUT THIS TIME …

Because he was over the moon, unbelievably,
undeniably, indescribably ecstatic over BAND!!

Finally, next week came and for once in a LONGGGGG time, Kered couldn't wait to get out of bed!

He couldn't wait to brush his teeth!

He couldn't wait to take a bath!

He couldn't wait to eat breakfast!!

AND he couldn't wait to go to …

SCHOOL!!!!!!!!

YES!!!!!!!!!!

The time had come for his first band rehearsal or practice, and Kered practically ran all the way to the bandroom.

He sat down in a seat, took out his shiny, new trumpet and began tooting a few notes ... as best he could.

Suddenly, out of the corner of his eye, he noticed someone sit down next to him.

IT WAS TONY!!!!!

"Hey, sissy! Gonna try and play the trumpet??? Ha! Puny, little thing like you can't even blow out a candle let alone blow a trumpet! Hahahahaha!!!"

"Wh-wh-what are you doing here?" Kered couldn't believe it!!!

"Well, my mom is making me. And my dad thought the trumpet would be a good instrument for me. I didn't want to join. But now that I see you're here, this is gonna be fun!"

Before any trouble could start, Mr. Kelly, the band director, entered the room and took his place at the podium in front of the class. He began explaining to the class that in a few weeks after everyone had gotten used to their instruments and he had a chance to teach them the basics of how to play, they would have shakedowns (or auditions) for chair positions to see who would sit where in the section.

Kered didn't know if he wanted to be there in a few weeks because of Tony. Suddenly, he didn't want to be there at all.

That night when his parents asked how his first day of band went, the first words out of Kered's mouth were:

"I want to QUIT!"
"QUIT??!" Everyone exclaimed!!

"But why??" Dad asked.

"I just want to." Was Kered's feeble reply.

"Okay. Something has been going on for a long time now, and I want you to tell us what it is." Mom demanded.

Kered said absolutely nothing.

Nicole decided to spill the beans.

"I think I know what it is. My friend Tracy Turner has a little brother in Kered's class, and he told her that he has seen Tony Roberts picking on Kered."

"That Tommy Turner has a big mouth!" Kered yelled!

Mom looked at Kered. "Is this true?"

You could barely hear Kered's reply. "Yes."

Dad stated, "So, that's why you have been so sad and not eating."

"I think we should speak with this Tony Roberts's parents." Mom stated.

But Nicole had a more direct approach.

"I think Kered should hit him!"

"NO HITTING!! That just makes things worse." Said Dad.

"Maybe Kered should prove he's a better trumpet player than Tony."

Everyone stared at Kimberly in utter disbelief.

"Well, maybe the best way to beat him is to … well, beat him at music. Be a better trumpet player. If he's going to play that thing, he may as well be good at it!"

Everybody still sat in silence, shocked over Kimberly's words. Then suddenly everyone burst into earsplitting laughter!

"That's a great idea! Dad was excited.

"Really? Do you think I can do it?" asked Kered.

"Of course you can! You just have to believe and know you can!" Mom was excited too.

Nicole replied, "Yeah, and practice like I do on my clarinet!"

"Well, then I'll start practicing right now!" Kered ran off to his bedroom and did just that – started practicing.

But poor Kimberly only had this to say: "Me and my big mouth."

Everyone laughed at that, too.

So, Kered practiced.

And practiced.

And practiced some more!

EVERY. DAY.

After weeks of band class – and Kered practicing A LOT on his own – Mr. Kelly announced it was time for shakedowns or auditions for the chair positions – to see who was the better player.

Kered was jittery, yet thrilled at the same time.

"You other trumpet players had better watch out, because I am going to get 1ˢᵗ chair!!" Tony boasted – and very loudly, too.

"We'll see about that," Kered mumbled under his breath.

The following week, Mr. Kelly began the auditions.

Monday and Tuesday would be the woodwind instruments. In other words, the flutes, clarinets, and saxophones were up first.

Wednesday would be the drums and percussion instruments.

Thursday would be the brass instruments, including the trombones, the French Horns and finally on Friday the rest of the brass, including the trumpets.

Each day listening to all the other instruments audition seemed to pass very, very slowly – which made Kered more and more nervous.

But each day after school, Kered practiced, practiced and practiced some more!!

Friday
FINALLY
arrived!!!

Everyone in the trumpet section would have their chance to audition, including Kered and Tony.

Tony played first. He actually sounded pretty good. That made Kered even more nervous. When Tony was done, he had this superior smirk on his face like he had won. Then Kered played. He thought he sounded okay, but he wasn't sure. When he had finished playing, Tony made a face like a bug had flown into his mouth and he had eaten it by mistake.

Afterward, all the other trumpet players played. Kered felt that out of all of them, Tony actually played the best.

But had he played better than Kered?

By now, everybody in the entire band had had a chance to audition for Mr. Kelly. Therefore, Mr. Kelly would soon announce the results, which meant even MORE waiting.

Since the trumpets had auditioned last, it was easy for Mr. Kelly to announce all of the results that day.

And so, Mr. Kelly began telling the woodwinds their results and where they would be sitting in order.

Then he did the same with the percussion and drums.

And last but not least, the brass section – beginning with the trombones, then the French horns, and finally – the trumpets.

There were, as to be expected, groans of disappointment mixed with little shouts of excitement as Mr. Kelly went through each section announcing who would be sitting where.

When Mr. Kelly got to the trumpet section, Kered tensed up. It was as if time had stopped. Mr. Kelly shuffled some papers until he came to the trumpet section. The shuffling of papers made Kered want to throw up. He felt as if the temperature in the room had skyrocketed to 200 degrees!! He could feel his ears throbbing and pounding as if the blood suddenly raced there. Oh how he wanted to pass out!

Then Mr. Kelly began – "First chair goes to ...

KERED RICHARDS!!!!!!!

Kered was speechless as everyone applauded ! Well, everyone except Tony, who for the first time looked very, very sad, especially when Mr. Kelly announced that he was 10th chair!!!

Mr. Kelly congratulated everyone on their hard work, but encouraged everyone to practice to do better the next time.

At the end of band class, Tony walked up to Kered. Kered braced himself for trouble. Looking down and obviously hard for him to say, Tony muttered "Congratulations, Kered. You really are the best trumpet player."

A shocked Kered could only mutter, "Thanks, Tony."

Tony then slowly started to walk away. Kered thought a minute before he finally said, "Hey, wait a minute, Tony. Would you like to practice together sometime?"

Tony looked up very surprised. "Yeah, yeah. Sure. Do you mean it?"

"Yes, sure." Kered replied.

"Hey, Kered. I'm really sorry I called you all those names. Anybody who can play as good as you can isn't a sissy."

Kered could only laugh. "Thanks, Tony!"

So, in the end not only did Kered get 1st chair of the trumpet section, but he also gained a new friend. They practiced together and eventually Tony ended up 2nd chair next to Kered.

(But he never, ever did beat Kered)

The

END

ABOUT THE AUTHOR

W. Derek Ratliff is a North Carolina native and 1990 graduate of the University of North Carolina at Chapel Hill. He has been in the Atlanta area for the past 28 years. He currently works at Emory University School of Medicine as a Standardized Patient and Event Assistant. He resides in Clarkston, Georgia. He has been acting since 1994, and has enjoyed doing theatre, film, infomercials, industrials, and TV. He was awarded a best actor award in 2001 for the theatrical production of "Early One Evening at The Rainbow Bar & Grille," for lead actor. He has written several children's plays that were produced, directed, and acted at the Children's Museum of Atlanta between 2007 and 2014. He is currently writing and producing his own web series entitled "Fabulous and Gorgeous."

ABOUT THE ILLUSTRATOR

Courtney Alexander Mosley was raised in Athens Georgia and won 2nd place in his first drawing contest at the age of six. In grade school, Courtney won various drawing contests, as well as creating his own comic strips which included many of his classmates and teachers as feature characters.

Courtney attended Athens Technical College where he studied Drafting and Design, and the Art Institute of Atlanta, where he studied Visual Communications specializing in Ad Design.

Courtney enjoys cartoon illustration and painting with acrylics on canvas. In 2009 he founded C. ALEXANDER DESIGNS. His masterpiece "The United Dream of America"© has been acknowledged by Congressman John Lewis and the staff of the 44th President of the United States Barack Obama.

Made in the USA
Coppell, TX
05 March 2021

51337089R00040